Chris Gets Ear Tubes

by Betty Pace

illustrations by Kathryn Hutton

Kendall Green Publications
Gallaudet University Press
Washington, D.C.

Kendall Green Publications
An imprint of Gallaudet University Press
Washington, DC 20002

Library of Congress Cataloging-in-Publication Data
Betty Pace, 1941–
    Chris gets ear tubes / Betty Pace.
        p. cm.
    Summary: Describes the experience of a young boy whose chronic ear
infections are affecting his hearing, until he goes into the hospital for a simple
operation.
    ISBN 0-930323-36-X
    1. Otitis media in children—Prevention—Juvenile literature. 2.Otitis media
in children—Surgery—Juvenile literature. [1. Otitis media. 2. Ear—Diseases.
3. Hospitals. 4. Medical care.] I. Title.
    RF225.P33 1987
    617.8 4059—dc19   87-26759
                                                                                 CIP
                                                                                  AC

*Special thanks to Dr. Laurie Thomas, ENT, and
Dr. Douglas Knoop, ENT, for their help and guidance.*

Gallaudet University is an equal opportunity employer/educational institution.
Programs and services offered by Gallaudet University receive substantial
financial support from the U.S. Department of Education.

To my husband Don

Chris was having trouble with his ears. He just couldn't hear right.

No one wanted to play with him in school because every time the teacher said something, Chris would always shout, **"What?"**

Chris's doctor had given him medicine to try to make his ears hear better, but the medicine didn't work.

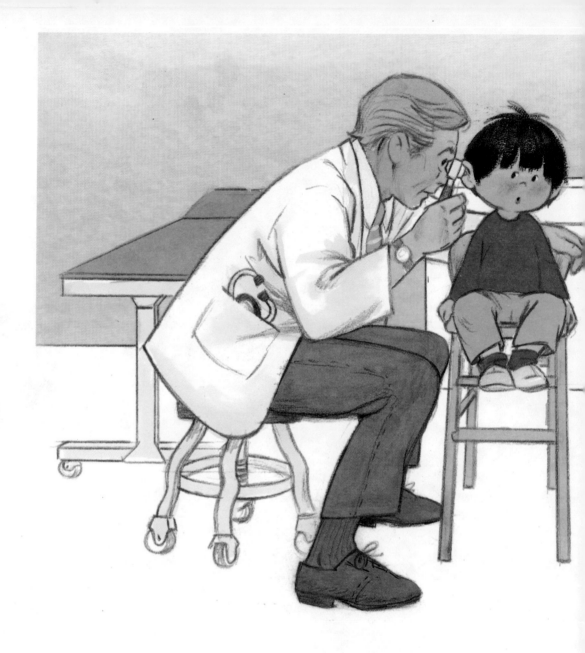

Dr. Lowe decided Chris needed a different kind of help.
"Chris, your ears should be dry inside, but they're not," he said. "There's something sticky inside them. The sticky stuff makes it hard for the noises to get through. When the noises can't get through, you can't hear very well."

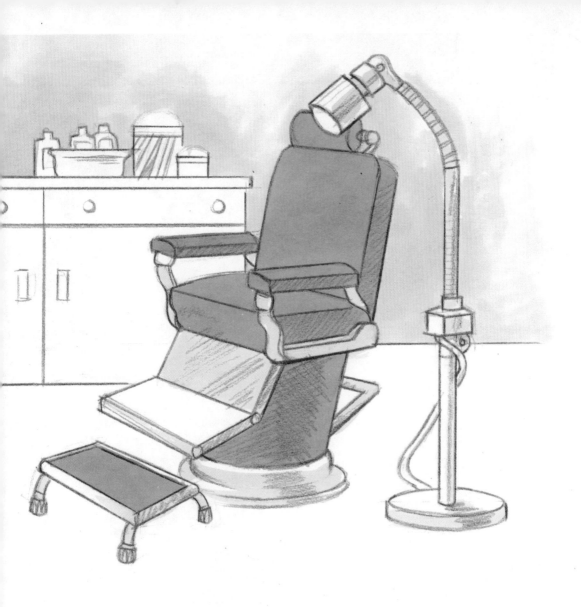

"Can you get the sticky stuff out?" asked Chris.

"Yes," answered Dr. Lowe. "I can put tiny tubes inside your ears. The tubes will take the sticky stuff out and make your ears stay dry."

Chris thought about that and said, "But my mom said I should never put anything into my ears."

"Your mother is right, Chris," answered Dr. Lowe, "and I'm glad you know that. Only a doctor should ever put anything inside your ears."

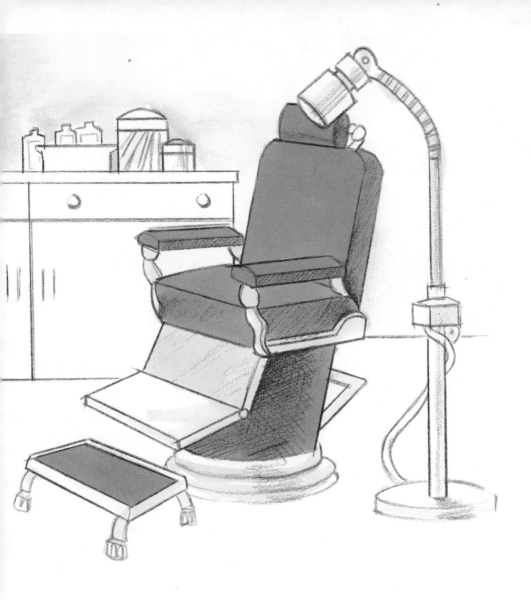

Chris thought some more, then asked, "Dr. Lowe, will you put tubes in right now?"

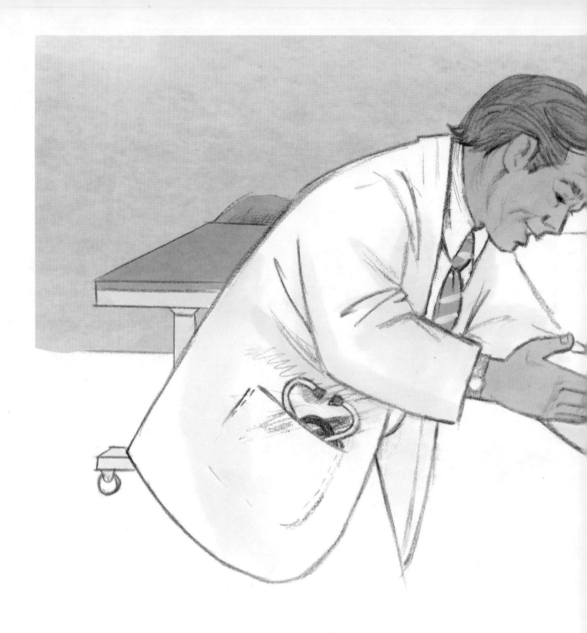

Dr. Lowe explained that putting in tubes was a kind of operation, so Chris would have to go to the hospital to get them. Chris didn't like the sound of that. He had heard about operations before, and he knew they hurt. He didn't like the idea of having tubes sticking out of his ears, either.

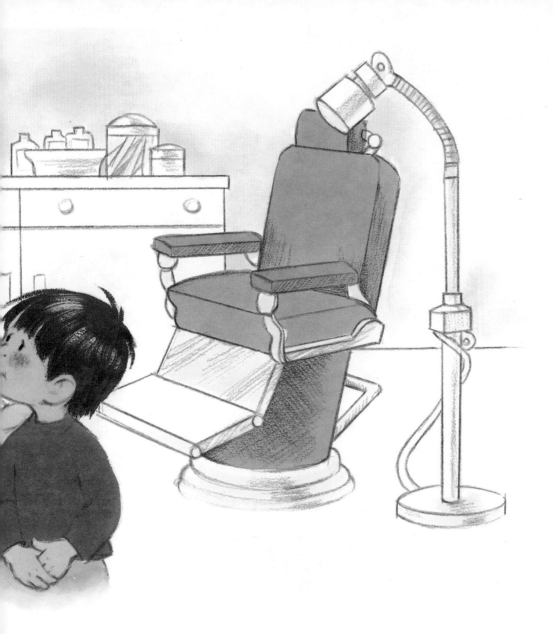

"Dr. Lowe, I'm really scared about this operation," said Chris.

"Most people are scared about operations," replied Dr. Lowe. "But this is a very small operation and it doesn't hurt at all. Many boys and girls get ear tubes every year."

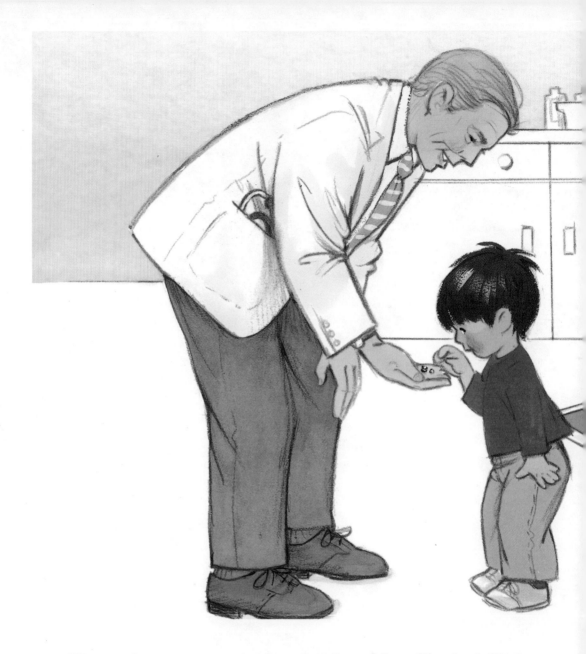

"Do you have some ear tubes that I could see?" asked Chris.
"Yes," said Dr. Lowe.

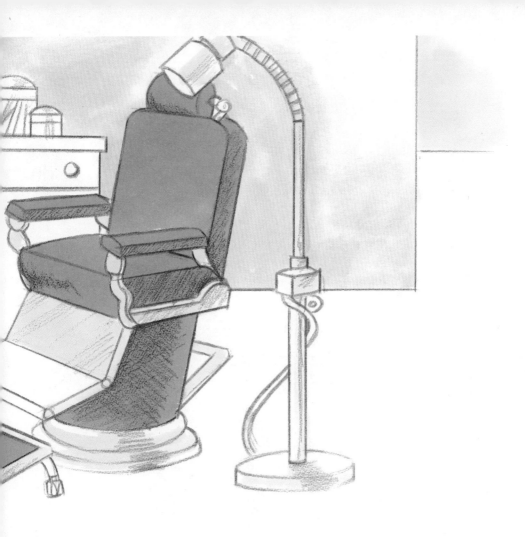

Dr. Lowe showed Chris some ear tubes and explained that they would be so far inside his ears that no one would be able to see them.

"You and your mother can come to the hospital early Thursday morning," Dr. Lowe said. "When you get there, a nurse will ask you some questions. She'll take your temperature, and feel your pulse, and listen to your heart and lungs.

Then she'll take your blood pressure and check your height and weight. When the nurse is through, we'll give you some medicine to let you sleep while I put the ear tubes in."

"Will I hear better when I get the tubes?" Chris asked.
"You sure will," said Dr. Lowe.
"Yea!" replied Chris. "Wait until I tell my friends."

Dr. Lowe talked about things to do the night before Chris's operation.

"Chris, you will not be allowed to eat anything after dinner," said Dr. Lowe.

"Not even a cookie?" asked Chris.

"That's right," said Dr. Lowe, "and on the day of surgery you cannot have any breakfast."

When Chris returned home, his friend Steve came over to play. Chris told Steve about his operation.

"Let's play Doctor," said Steve.

"Okay," said Chris. "I'll be the doctor and you be the kid getting ear tubes."

The day finally arrived for Chris's surgery. His mother
and father took him to the hospital early that morning. Chris
met Mrs. Baker, the admissions clerk.

Mrs. Baker asked him some questions, then she put a
bracelet on his arm.

"Why are you putting that on me?" Chris asked.

"Hospitals use bracelets so people will know who you are,"
said Mrs. Baker. "See, your bracelet tells us that your name is
Chris, that you're going to be in room 5, and that Dr. Lowe
will be taking care of you."

"Oh!" said Chris. "I guess the bracelet will tell everyone who I am if I get lost."

"That's right," Mrs. Baker replied. "Everyone will know who you are, even when you're sleeping."

Chris guided his mother and father to the elevator. When they arrived on the children's floor, they met Miss Hall.

"Hello, Chris," Miss Hall said. "I'm going to be your nurse today."

Miss Hall showed Chris to his room and gave him a
hospital gown to wear. Chris liked the gown.

"Wait until Dr. Lowe sees my gown," said Chris. "He will
really like the circus animals on it."

"Dr. Lowe will be wearing a gown, too," said Miss Hall.
"Will Dr. Lowe's gown have circus animals on it?" asked Chris.
"Oh, no," replied Miss Hall. "Dr. Lowe and all the nurses
will be wearing green gowns during your operation."

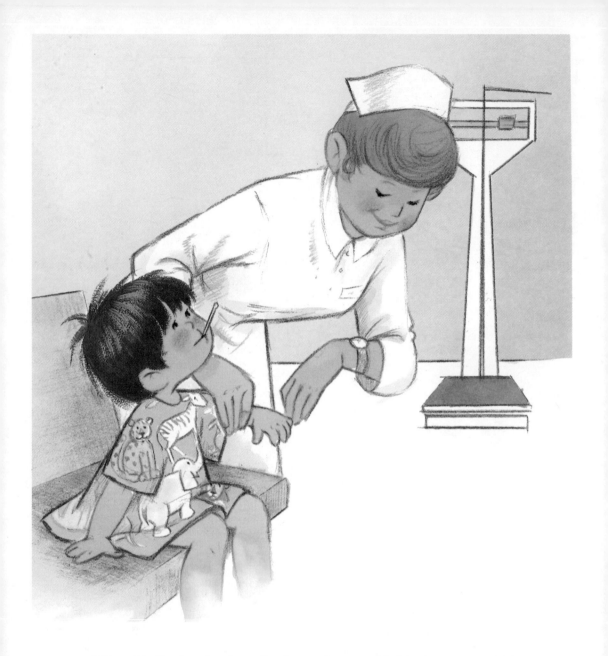

Miss Hall checked to find out how tall Chris was and how much he weighed. She took his temperature and felt his pulse. "You are a healthy boy," she said. "You will do just fine today."

"Is it time for my operation?" Chris asked.

"Not yet," answered Miss Hall. "First I must show you one
of the most important places in this hospital."

"What is it?" Chris asked.

"The playroom," Miss Hall replied.

"You can stay here until Dr. Lowe is ready for you. Would you like to play now?"

"Okay!" Chris said happily.

Chris played for a long time. "I really like it here," he said. "I wish I could stay here all the time instead of having an operation."

Just when Chris started thinking about being hungry, Miss Hall came to get him for his operation.

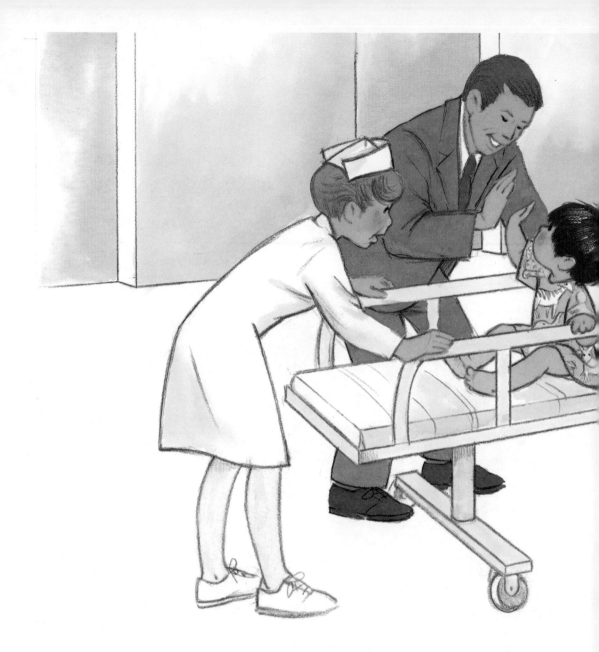

Miss Hall put Chris on a bed that had sides like a baby's crib. She explained that she wanted to be sure Chris didn't roll out of bed when he fell asleep. Chris's mother gave him a big hug and he and his father slapped a five.

Then Miss Hall pushed him down the hall to the operating room.

In the operating room, everyone had on masks and green gowns. Chris couldn't keep from laughing. "You all look like people from Outer Space," he said.

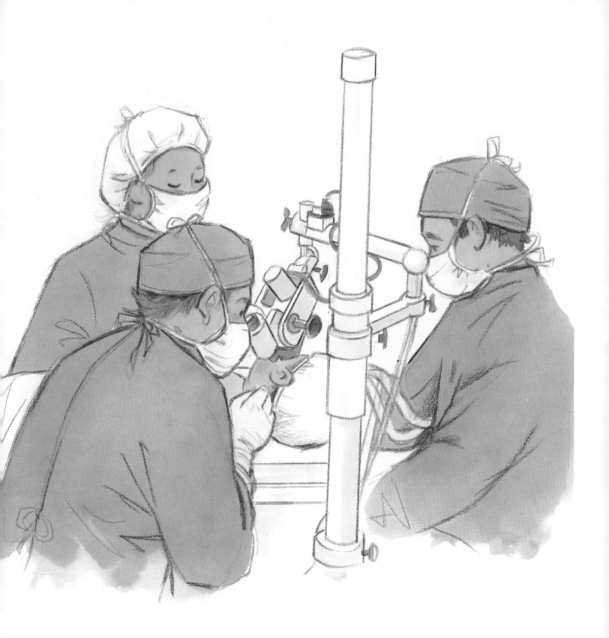

Dr. Lowe patted Chris on the shoulder. Then he gave Chris some medicine to make him sleep. While Chris was sleeping, Dr. Lowe made small holes in each of his eardrums. Then he got the sticky fluid out of Chris's ears, and he put a tiny plastic tube in each small hole.

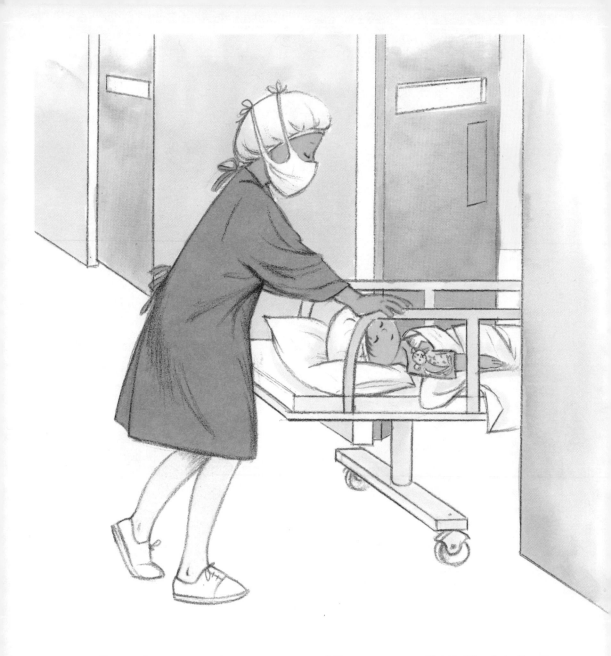

Soon the operation was over. The nurse rolled Chris's bed
to another room where she could watch him until he woke up.

Miss Hall told Chris's mother and father that the operation was over and Chris was doing fine.

Dr. Lowe came to talk to Chris's mother and father. "The tubes should stay in Chris's ears a long time," he said. "When the ears have healed, the tubes will fall out."

"Can Chris go swimming?" asked Chris's father.

"Oh, yes," answered Dr. Lowe. "We can make ear plugs for his ears when he comes back for his check-up."

When Chris was wide awake, Miss Hall brought him back
to his room. His mother and father were waiting for him.

Chris was glad to see his parents, but he really wanted
something to drink. Miss Hall brought Chris a cup of juice.

After Chris drank the juice, he said, "Guess what, Mom and Dad. Dr. Lowe was right. It didn't hurt at all when he put the tubes in my ears."

"That's terrific!" replied his father.

"And guess what else, I can hear much better."
"That's even better," his mother said.
"Can I go home now?" Chris asked.
"Yes, as soon as you get dressed, we can go home."

Chris said good-bye to the nurses.

He gave Miss Hall a special hug.
"How are you feeling?" she asked.
"I feel great," Chris said, "and I can hear much better
already. I'm going to tell my friends all about my tubes."

The next day at school Chris could hear every word the teacher said.

His friends were happy because he didn't have to shout
"What" anymore. They all wanted to play with him.

What a difference it made to be able to hear well again!